SOLDIER'S COURAGE

A SWEET MILITARY ROMANCE

HONOR VALLEY ROMANCES
BOOK THREE

SHANAE JOHNSON

THOSE JOHNSON GIRLS

CHAPTER ONE

Grace Montgomery stepped into the library, a sense of calm and familiarity washing over her. The scent of books, a comforting blend of ink and paper, filled the air. Sunlight streamed through the windows, casting a warm glow on the rows of shelves.

With a practiced ease, Grace moved through the library, straightening books and adjusting displays. Her fingers trailed along the spines as if greeting old friends. Each book held its own story, a world waiting to be explored. The thought made her heart swell with a deep appreciation for the magic within these walls.

She reached for a feather duster and delicately

swept away the dust that had settled overnight. Mrs. Jordan, the former librarian, had told the tale that fairies snuck in at night and left behind their dust. It was just another story that had sparked Grace's imagination as a child and made her fall in love with this magical place. As the soft bristles glided over the shelves, she couldn't help but smile. The library was her sanctuary, a place where imagination flourished and dreams took flight.

Grace moved to the circulation desk, organizing paperwork and checking her calendar. She admired the colorful posters promoting upcoming events, from book clubs to children's story time. The library was more than just a building filled with books; it was a community hub, a place where connections were made and knowledge was shared.

As the clock ticked closer to opening time, Grace made her way to the entrance, unlocking the doors. She paused for a moment, taking in the stillness of the library before the rush of patrons. It was in these quiet moments that she felt a sense of purpose, knowing that she was providing a haven for book lovers, young and old.

Grace flipped the sign from "Closed" to "Open." The doors swung wide, inviting the world inside.

She felt a thrill of anticipation. Who would walk through those doors today? What stories would be discovered, what lives would be touched?

Only a soft breeze whistled by at nine in the morning. The streets were empty with just a few stragglers rushing into doors, trying not to be too late. With the workday in full swing and summer school in session, Grace knew better than to expect anybody for at least a couple of hours.

It was the perfect time to pick up where she left off in her latest novel. Grace sat behind the circulation desk, lost in the pages of Evelyn Rivers' latest fantasy romance novel. The words whisked her away to a world of love and adventure, her heart racing alongside the characters she had grown to adore. She relished these stolen moments, indulging in the passion and magic woven between the lines.

As she turned a page, a movement caught her attention. A tall figure entered the library. The height was notable because most people in town weren't as tall as Grace. The high school basketball coach had begged her to join his team until he saw Grace's utter lack of coordination.

Coordination wasn't the only game Grace lacked. She had decidedly poor skills when it came to the opposite sex. She took most of her cues from Sweet Valley High novels and Harlequins, a language not one single teenage boy in the world spoke. Add that to her height disadvantage, and Grace's dating life was dustier than the bookshelves each morning.

The man who walked In the door was easily a few inches taller than her, maybe a whole foot. His features were partially concealed beneath the shadow of his cap. Grace's curiosity was piqued, but she respected his desire for solitude. She knew that the library could be a sanctuary for those seeking solace, just as it was for her.

He strode through the aisles, his steps quiet yet purposeful. Grace's eyes followed him discreetly, a flicker of intrigue dancing within her. He stopped in the Classics section; British Classics, to be exact. The tall figure stood amongst Hardy, Dickens, Orwell.

She watched as he pulled out a book, his fingers tracing the pages with gentle reverence. Grace's eyes narrowed, her desire to know the title of the book growing stronger. She leaned forward, trying to catch a glimpse of the cover, but her view remained obstructed. It was as if the universe conspired to keep his chosen read hidden from her prying eyes.

The doors to the library opened again. But this time, it was a short man with his head tilted back in an air of importance. Grace begrudgingly put her book down to greet Councilman Spalding. As the head of the town council, he was technically her boss.

Grace rose from her desk as Mr. Spalding entered the library, a cloud of unease lingering around him. She couldn't help but notice his narrowed eyes and the way he discreetly waved his hand in front of his face, as though trying to ward off an invisible enemy. It seemed as if he were either allergic to dust or, heaven forbid, allergic to the very essence of the books that surrounded them.

"Good morning, Mr. Spalding." Grace greeted him with a warm smile, despite the foreboding feeling creeping up her spine. "How can I help you today?"

Mr. Spalding cleared his throat, his discomfort evident. "Grace, I'm here with some news that I believe you'll find rather troubling."

Grace said nothing. Her mother had told her that Mr. Spalding had been a part of the drama team back when they were in school. He'd returned to Honor's Valley after a failed career on Broadway.

Mr. Spalding took a deep breath. "As you know, the council is looking to trim the budget. The library is an important part of the community, and we all want to protect it. But we do have to make some adjustments. To that end, there are proposed cuts to the reading program."

Grace's heart skipped a beat. She'd been prepared for her acquisitions budget to get decimated, but she had a plan for that. Or perhaps they'd cut one of the two assistants she had, which would have been devastating, but she would've pulled double shifts.

The reading program was not just a collection of books and activities—it was a lifeline for the children in their community. It provided them with opportunities to explore new worlds, expand their horizons, and develop a lifelong love of reading. Cutting it would be a devastating blow.

"You're going after the children's program?"

Mr. Spalding's carefully constructed façade faltered.

"I can't accept that, Mr. Spalding," she said firmly. "The reading program is an invaluable resource for our children. It instills a love of learning and helps them discover the power of their own imaginations. We must fight to keep it intact."

Mr. Spalding shifted uncomfortably, his eyes flickering with a mix of surprise and uncertainty. "Grace, you know the budget constraints we're facing," he said, his tone apologetic. "There are other priorities to consider."

"Our children are our future, Mr. Spalding." Now she was the one being dramatic, but Whitney Houston had it right. "We owe it to them to invest in their education and their dreams. We can find ways to make this work, to secure the funding and support needed to preserve the reading program. I won't let it be taken away without a fight."

"You can bring it up at the next council meeting, but I can't see any other way that won't affect cutting personnel."

Grace felt a surge of frustration. She had been fighting to get the reading program installed for months. Now they were going to take it away. The head of the council might not see the value in the program or might not have received any significant support or feedback from the community. They might see the program as a low priority and not worth fighting for. But Grace knew better.

She had seen firsthand the impact that the reading program had on the children in the community, and she refused to let it go without a fight.

CHAPTER TWO

ason sat at a table in the corner of the library, lost in thought. He traced his fingers over the cover of a novel, trying to distract himself from the memories that haunted him. The physical scars had healed, but the emotional wounds were still raw and tender.

He found some solace in the cozy corner of the library, his sanctuary amidst the rows of books. The pages of *Far from the Madding Crowd* transported him to a world far removed from the chaos and noise that surrounded him. He relished the peace he found within those pages, where the fictional lives and loves captured his imagination.

As he read, he kept sneaking glances at the pretty librarian whose head was also bowed over a novel. Though Mason knew she kept sneaking glances at him. Of course she did. He was a horror show now.

His fingers left the worn pages of the novel and reached for his face. A wave of unease washed over him, reminding him of his injury and the emotional scars that ran deep. Months had passed since his return from duty, but the wounds, both seen and unseen, still lingered. The thought of venturing out into the world, exposing himself to scrutiny and potential judgment, sent tremors of anxiety through his veins. He had always been more comfortable within the pages of a book than in the company of others, even before his injury.

A part of him yearned for connection, for the possibility of finding acceptance and understanding in another's eyes. But fear held him back, the fear of being vulnerable, of being seen for who he truly was beneath the armor he had built around himself. It was easier to retreat into the fictional worlds where happy endings were guaranteed, where love and acceptance were always within reach.

At least in this particular Hardy novel the characters found acceptance. Throughout the narrative, the heroine navigates the complexities of love, loyalty, and personal growth. In the end, she realizes her true feelings for the humble and steadfast shepherd who had loved her from the beginning. The novel concludes with the lovers coming together, finding mutual understanding, and embracing a future filled with love and happiness. Their union represented a harmonious resolution, offering readers a satisfying and optimistic conclusion.

Mason didn't see that same ending for himself. He should be happy that there were still pages of his story to be told. Though he suspected much of his future would be written in the shadows now.

Lost in thought, he returned his focus to the novel, allowing the familiar words to envelop him once more. The characters became his companions, their triumphs and heartaches intertwining with his own. In the world of literature, Mason found a refuge where he could be himself without fear of judgment.

Mason's eyes lifted from the pages of his book, momentarily distracted by the sound of Grace's voice carrying the weight of distress. She stood toe to toe with a foe. But she had a good foot on the man.

Still, Mason listened, his instincts as a

protector stirring within him. For a fleeting moment, the familiar urge to rush to her aid surged through his veins, the remnants of his past identity as a soldier were still etched upon his soul.

Reality crashed over him like a wave, reminding him of the scars, both visible and invisible, that marked his journey. He was no longer the unwavering hero he once believed himself to be. He had been wounded, not only physically, but emotionally, burdened by the weight of a loss he couldn't shake.

He had nothing to offer her in this moment. He doubted he could truly make a difference. The wounds he carried, the guilt that weighed him down, whispered doubts in his ear, convincing him that he was no longer capable of being the hero he'd once aspired to be.

Reluctantly, Mason's shoulders slumped, his desire to spring into action slowly dissipating. Resigned, Mason returned his gaze to the pages of the book before him, his heart heavy with the weight of his own perceived inadequacies. He couldn't bear to let anyone see the brokenness within him, the doubts that threatened to consume him. So he remained in his corner of the library, a solitary figure lost between the lines of his own story.

As he sat lost in thought, he heard the sound of footsteps approaching. He looked up to see his niece, Emily, walking toward him with a book in her hands. Her eyes were downcast, and she seemed to be trying to hide something.

"Hey, Uncle Mason. Can we go and get ice cream?"

"I already fell for that, and your mom read me the riot act."

"What's the riot act?"

"You're in a library, kiddo. You can read about it yourself."

Emily shrugged, her cheeks turning pink. "Never mind," she said quietly.

It wasn't the first time she'd avoided reading. When he'd come to stay with his sister and her husband after he separated from the military, Mason had brought along some of his favorite children's books for his niece. They all sat on the bookshelf in her bedroom with each spine uncracked.

"I'll make a deal with you, kiddo. Homework. Then ice cream."

That should have won him a grin. Instead,

Emily pursed her lips. She took her time unzipping her backpack and taking out her textbooks and worksheets from summer school. The classes were only a few hours a day, leaving her to get out of school earlier than both her parents left work. That's where Mason stepped in. He watched Emily for that gap of time, and unfortunately for her, he preferred to spend that time in the library.

Mason noted that Emily took out her math sheets first. Those were completed quickly, and by his furtive glances, they all looked correct. Then out came the reading comprehension worksheets, where he saw Emily struggling.

"Wow," he said peering over at the paper "Is that what they're giving you in second grade? That looks incredibly hard."

"It is." Emily hesitated, her finger tracing the sentence, her voice laced with frustration. "I don't know this word, Uncle Mason."

Mason placed a hand gently on her shoulder. "Looks like they're giving you pretty big words. Let's break it down. What sounds do you recognize?"

Some of the tension relaxed in her small shoulders as he helped her to dissect the word, sounding out each letter.

"You're doing great," he praised, his voice filled with genuine pride. "Now, let's think about what the word could mean in the context of the sentence."

Mason offered gentle prompts and guidance, ensuring that Emily felt supported rather than overwhelmed. He understood the weight that young minds carried, the desire to excel and the fear of falling short. He was determined to create an environment where Emily felt safe to learn and make mistakes.

At times, he caught a glimpse of frustration flickering in her eyes, a shadow of guilt for not grasping the concepts as quickly as she wished. Mason's voice softened as he leaned closer, his words carrying the weight of unconditional love for the little pipsqueak.

When he glanced up, he caught the librarian eying the two of them with wide eyes. Mason hadn't realized that he'd taken his cap off at some point. But the librarian wasn't looking at the scar that ran down the length of his cheek. Her gaze flickered between him, Emily, and the papers between them.

"Okay, kiddo, that's enough for now. Let's go grab that ice cream."

Mason shoved his cap back on his head. He tugged it down low as he rose and gathered Emily's backpack. He ushered the little girl out of the library as quickly as possible without a glance back.

But he should have been looking ahead. The librarian had posted herself in front of the door. She stood there with the hugest grin. And it was directed at him.

CHAPTER THREE

Grace knew Emily Wallace. The little girl used to come in all the time with her mother and spend hours in the picture books section. But Grace hadn't seen her for at least a year.

The man holding Emily's hand was the spitting image of her but with a dark beard covering his chin and a hat dipped low on his head. It was the eyes. Those bright green eyes that were filled with equal parts inquisitiveness and wisdom.

This man wasn't Emily's father. Grace had grown up with Rich Wallace. He'd married a woman from out of town, one he'd met in college. Mary Ellen was her name. Grace had really liked Mary Ellen, though the two didn't hang out much after Mary Ellen became a mom. She did remember Mary Ellen mentioning a brother. This must be him.

"Hi, I'm Grace." Grace extended her hand.

Mary Ellen's brother stared at her hand like it could be an explosive device or some other weapon bent on taking him down. Grace remembered Mary Ellen had mentioned that her brother was deployed. He certainly had the countenance of a soldier.

Whenever he came into the library, he always sat facing the door. He never slumped in the chair. He always sat up straight. His face was serious as he turned the pages of the book, as though he was studying a mission report.

"Hi, Ms. Montgomery," said Emily. "This is my Uncle Mason."

"It's nice to see you again, Emily. Hello, Mason."

Finally, Mason took her hand. Grace felt the heat of his fingertips before they made contact with her skin. She had a full second to brace herself before impact.

That second wasn't enough time.

Grace's heart fluttered in her chest as Mason's hand gently closed around hers. Time seemed to stand still in that fleeting moment, the world around them fading into insignificance. His touch sent a surge of electricity coursing through her veins.

Her breath caught in her throat as their eyes met, the intensity of his gaze igniting a spark deep within her. In that instant, she felt a profound connection, as if their paths were destined to intertwine. It was as if the pages of the countless romance novels she had devoured had come to life before her eyes, the promise of an epic love story unfolding right in front of her.

The weight of his hand in hers was both comforting and exhilarating, sending shivers of anticipation cascading down her spine. Grace's imagination ran wild, spinning a tapestry of possibilities. Could this be the start of something extraordinary, a love story that would defy all odds and sweep them both off their feet?

As an avid reader of romance novels, she had always longed for a meet-cute straight from the pages of her favorite books. And now standing before her was a man who seemed to embody every hero she had ever dreamed of.

In that charged moment, Grace couldn't help but wonder if their meeting was more than mere coincidence. It felt like the universe had aligned the stars, guiding them to this very instant. And as she stared into Mason's eyes, she realized that this connection held the promise of something profound and life-changing.

"I need to get you ready for bed," he said, his voice the deep timbre of one of the werewolves she read about on her Kindle.

"I beg your pardon?" Grace's voice was breathy as she spoke.

"Emily. I need to get her home and ready for bed."

"But Uncle Mason, it's afternoon. And you promised ice cream."

"That was before I realized how late it was. We need to get going."

Mason moved toward the door, but something held him in place. Looking down, they both became aware that they were still holding hands. He let go of hers as though it was indeed a bomb sizzling at the lit tip. But Grace still felt the sparks tingling up the inside of her arm.

He was affected, too. She could tell. His pupils were dilated. His nostrils flaring. And he was looking anywhere but at her.

"I need you," she said.

That got his attention. Mason looked up, those

green eyes latching on to hers in complete surprise and a hint of helpless vulnerability.

"I need your help," Grace corrected. Though in all honesty, she'd meant what she said the first time. "I think you heard what the councilman said about the reading program."

Mason shifted uncomfortably, breaking the eye contact.

Grace ducked her head until she caught his gaze again before she continued. "I just watched you with Emily."

Emily had ventured to the video games section, which was on the other side of the children's section of the library. With the little girl out of earshot, Grace felt comfortable speaking more on the struggles she'd just witnessed.

"The patience you have with her, the ingenuity, other kids need that."

Mason was already shaking his head. "I don't have time-"

"You'd make such a difference in these young kids' lives. Especially being a hero, a soldier they would look up to. Plus, I can already see you're a fan of the classics."

Grace pointed to the Thomas Hardy book in his hand. It wasn't Grace's type of romance, but at least it was one of the few classics that ended happily and without the heroine committing suicide or being shunned.

At least it wasn't *Tess of the D'Urbervilles.* Grace had picked up that book and gotten halfway through before realizing it was not going to have a happy ending. But being the completionist that she was, she trudged through. The novel told the tragic story of Tess Durbeyfield, a young woman from a working-class family who was manipulated and victimized by the higher social classes. In Hardy's classic need to explore themes of social injustice, fate, and the destructive power of society's expectations, he ended the novel as a tragedy instead of having the characters triumph. As a fan of fanfic, Grace had rewritten the ending to end happily with the lovers escaping the tendrils of the upper-class snare and living happily on a dairy farm.

Instead of the softening expression Grace had expected from her making a connection with his book, Mason's features hardened. He turned, giving her only his profile. "I'm sorry, but I can't help you."

"Are… are you sure?"

"Yes, I'm sorry. Em, let's grab that ice cream."

The little girl gave a cheer as she hurried back

over to her uncle. The two were out the door before Grace could get another word out. She watched them walk away, Emily skipping along and Mason with that stiff stride she'd witnessed in many of the soldiers who worked on the base.

Grace wasn't sure where she'd gone wrong with him. But after that spark that had ignited between them, she knew that she wasn't wrong. Mason would be the perfect person to help with the reading program at the library. His background in the military had given him a unique perspective, and his experience with his niece had given him the patience and skill to work with struggling readers.

He would be perfect for the job. She couldn't help but wonder if he'd also make the perfect boyfriend. Only time would tell, and Grace was determined to have another chance at both opportunities with Mason.

CHAPTER FOUR

Jason walked out of the library, his heart pounding in his chest. He couldn't believe that he had let his guard down like that, that he had shown Grace the one thing that he had been keeping hidden from the world.

He knew that he shouldn't feel ashamed of his love for romance novels, but he couldn't help it. It was something that he had always kept to himself, something that he had turned to in his darkest moments, when he was struggling with the memories of war and the pain of his injuries.

But the truth was that reading romance novels was one of the few things that brought him comfort, that helped him escape from the nightmares and the flashbacks. He liked the guaranteed endings, the promise of a happily ever after, something that he couldn't find in his own life.

As he walked down the street, the Hardy book still clutched in his hand. He'd forgotten to check it out. He'd have to go back lest he be labeled a thief as well as a grump who didn't want to help kids. He was embarrassed, and he didn't want to think about what Grace must be thinking of him now.

She'd also blatantly stared at his face. Even when he'd tried to turn away, to hide his scar, she'd still sought him out. He had no idea why he'd turned to her, displaying his wound in its fullness to her gaze.

Ice cream spilled into the crevices of his hand and palm, the cone of cream forgotten as he mulled over what had just taken place inside the hallowed halls of his safe place in town. He couldn't ever go back there.

"Uncle Mason, are you going to eat that?"

Without thought of consequences, Mason handed over the dripping cone to Emily. The little girl had already managed to talk him into a triple decker cone. And now she had added two more to her tower with his surrender.

Because that's what the last thirty minutes had felt like.

When Grace had sought him out after her encounter with the councilman, he'd felt like he'd been enlisted into a battle. When she'd stood in front of the door as he'd tried to retreat, he'd felt like he was about to be court-martialed for deserting. Even now, when he'd managed to separate himself from her, he felt like he was still under her command.

And then there had been that moment when they'd first touched.

He'd never felt that way with another woman. He'd only read about it in books. Things like that weren't supposed to happen in real life. And yet, he'd felt it—a spark.

It had to be one-sided. A woman like that could never feel something for a man like him. A scarred man who couldn't break free of the hold his demons had on him.

She just wanted him for her program. To help kids. But he couldn't do it. It was far too much exposure to be under her gaze, much less a bunch of rowdy kids who didn't want to learn.

"So you're gonna work at the library now?"

"What?" Mason turned to Emily, who was

licking chocolate cream from the center of her palm.

"I know some kids who have a hard time reading, like me. Maybe you could help them, too? If you worked at the library."

Despite teaching Emily a few new words today, Mason had no words for her now. At least none for what she was asking about at present. "Let's get you home."

If he'd known what was waiting for him at his sister's house, he would've done another about face and run.

"What were you thinking, Mace?"

Mary Ellen was a good foot shorter than her older brother, but she had had him wrapped around her finger since the day she was born.

"She's hopped up on sugar," she continued. "She definitely won't eat her veggies. And I know I'm going to have a time getting her to sleep tonight."

"Sorry, Mellie."

Instead of being read the riot act, which he both expected and deserved, his sister put a hand to his face. She'd been doing this ever since she was a baby. She'd put that chubby hand to his face, look into his eyes, and get him to spill all his thoughts.

"What's going on with you?"

Mason sighed.

"You were at the library?"

Mason nodded.

"Did you run into the librarian?" Mary Ellen grinned. "I was hoping you and Grace would meet and hit it off."

Mason reared back, but his baby sister held fast.

"You can't keep hiding, Mace. You're an amazing guy, and it's time for you to get out in the world. You could do a lot worse than Grace."

"Mellie-"

"Don't Mellie me. The two of you already have so much in common. Books for one. Why do you think I sent you there?"

Mason was used to her playing matchmaker. She'd tried to set him up with her teachers, her babysitter, and even one of her friend's older sisters. None of those took. But there was something about Grace.

"She wants me to help with the after school reading program."

"That would be perfect for you with your English lit degree."

"I don't know."

"Think about it. Hey, you owe me after you wrecked my kid for the night."

"Okay." Mason held up his hands. "I'll think about it."

He bent down and let her kiss him on the cheek —on his good side. Mellie was good about pretending not to see her brother's flaws. But Mason was not good about pretending they weren't there.

Even though he hadn't had any ice cream, he didn't feel the least bit tired. He took his book and headed back outside. By now the library was closed. Not that he would return to that scene tonight.

Instead, he went down to the beach. There was a park bench that was off to the side he'd found last weekend. He tucked into the bench and opened the pages. A sense of calm settled over him as he found his place in the story he loved so dearly.

As he turned the pages, Mason lost himself in the world of the story, the promise of a happy ending bringing him a sense of peace that he couldn't find anywhere else. Also, as he read, he thought of Grace, of the way she had tried to reach out to him, to understand him. He knew that he had been too grumpy with her, too quick to push her away.

His concentration was shattered when he overheard the conversation of people walking behind him.

"... and that's why I think we should cut funding for the reading program," said a voice that Mason recognized as Mr. Spalding, the head of the council.

"I don't know, Jenkins," said another voice. "The reading program has been a real success. The kids seem to be responding well to it."

"But at what cost?" said Mr. Spalding. "We're pouring resources into something that isn't producing any real results. I don't see the value in it, and I don't think the rest of the council does either."

Mason listened with growing frustration as Spalding coldly dismissed the importance of Grace's cherished reading program. The callousness in his words struck a nerve deep within Mason, igniting a fire of anger and indignation. Unable to contain his emotions any longer, Mason rose to his feet, filled with a mix of passion and fury.

"How can you be so heartless?" he challenged,

his words cutting through the air like a sharp blade.

Both men turned to him, startled by his sudden outburst. Mason's body trembled with the intensity of his emotions as he locked eyes with Mr. Spalding, determined to make him understand the gravity of his actions.

"I grew up with books as my escape, my refuge," Mason continued. "To deny these children the opportunity to discover that same solace, that same joy, is nothing short of cruel."

Mr. Spalding's face contorted into a mix of surprise and disdain as he glared back at Mason. "And who are you to question our decisions?" he retorted, his voice dripping with condescension. "Some scarred nobody who should keep to the shadows."

Mason felt the sting of Mr. Spalding's words like a knife to his heart. The scars, both physical and emotional, had long been a source of vulnerability for him, carrying the weight of his past battles and the burdens he had shouldered.

Anger flared within Mason, threatening to unleash a torrent of fury in response to Mr. Spalding's heartless remark. He rose to his full height, which left him towering over the man who was small in stature and personality. With a yelp, Spalding and his companion hurried away from Mason's imposing figure.

With his heart still pounding, Mason took a deep breath, trying to regain his composure. He realized that his anger, while justified, needed to be channeled into productive action.

It looked like the end of the reading program was a done deal by the sounds of that conversation. But Mason refused to take that result sitting down. He was already on his feet, and he wouldn't stand by and watch as that small-minded man dismantled the program and robbed the children of the chance to learn and grow. He knew that he had to do something to save the reading program.

CHAPTER FIVE

Grace stepped out of the library, the weight of the day still lingering on her shoulders. Aria and Sarah were waiting for her at their usual meeting spot in Sandy Perk, the best coffee shop in town. The warm aroma of freshly brewed coffee enveloped her as she entered, mingling with the lively chatter of patrons and the soft melody playing in the background.

Her friends greeted her with smiles, their enthusiasm infectious. Aria's curly hair bounced with every excited gesture, while Sarah's eyes sparkled with the warmth of new love. Both women had met their matches recently and were happily in the throes of new love.

Grace didn't want to burst their love bubbles,

but she had to tell them what had gone down in the library earlier. The upsetting bit, not the bit about scaring off a potential suitor of her own. And so she took a deep breath, her voice filled with urgency as she began sharing the news.

"You won't believe what the town council is planning."

Her friends looked at her expectantly. Aria handed over a warm cup of chamomile with a dash of oat milk before settling in her seat.

"They want to get rid of the after-school reading program."

Aria gasped, her expressive face a canvas of outrage. "You can't be serious. How could they even consider such a thing?"

"The library is where I found my love for exotic flowers," said Sarah. "We can't let this happen. The kids need a program like this."

Grace nodded, her determination ignited by the unwavering support of her friends. She knew that together, with their collective voices, they could make a difference that would resonate through the chambers of the town council. But they needed more people. It would be even better if they had a backup who could help the kids in case the council got its way.

"You won't believe who I talked to today," Grace said, a hint of a smile playing at the corner of her lips.

"Broody Book Boy?" said Aria.

Grace winced at the name they'd given Mason before they knew who he was. "He has a name."

"He told you his name?" squealed Sarah. "Is it something based on the British classics he has an appreciation for?"

"It's Mason, Mason Anderson. He's Mary Ellen's brother."

"Oh, I know her," said Aria. "She's in here every Sunday morning for peppermint hot chocolate with sprinkles and whip cream."

Sarah's eyes sparkled with curiosity. "Tell us more, Grace. What did he say?"

"I blew it." Grace sighed. "I pounced on him about helping out with the reading program after I saw how he helped little Emily Wallace."

"Ahhh," her softie girlfriends chimed in unison.

"Then, I pointed out that I saw him reading a romance novel, and he got all weird. I think I embarrassed him."

"Because he reads romance novels?" asked Sarah. "What woman wouldn't want to date a man who read the definitive manual to our hearts?"

"Well, technically it wasn't a romance novel." At least not by her standards.

Grace wanted to tell them more. She wanted to tell them about the spark she'd felt when their fingers brushed. She wanted to tell them about the way her heart had skipped when their gazes met. She wanted to tell them that she'd felt her world shift after the first words he'd spoken directly to her. But because he'd walked away from her, she doubted it was the beginning of a great love story.

He hadn't even agreed to help her out when he witnessed her as a damsel in distress. So instead, she lifted her mug and listened as her two best friends went on about their new boyfriends and the romantic gestures they performed for them.

Grace entered the library early the next morning, her arms full of books and her mind buzzing with plans to save the reading program. Aside from cooing over their love lives, Aria and Sarah had brainstormed a number of ideas about the program as well as which neighbors to talk to for support. The three women were determined to save the program, no matter what it took. And with her friends on her side, the council didn't know what they were up against.

Grace carefully slid a book onto the shelf, her mind absorbed in the task at hand. The library was quiet. Its hallowed halls were filled with the gentle whispers of pages. As Grace set the books down on the front desk, she heard the sound of footsteps behind her. She turned around to see Mason walking through the door.

It wasn't his usual time. She knew that because she'd clocked his movements over the last seven days. Besides, Grace had thought she'd scared him away.

"Good morning," she said.

"Morning." Mason stood by one of the bookshelves, his broad shoulders tense and his gaze averted.

"Can I help you find something?" she asked, walking over to him.

He held up a book. It was the Hardy novel from yesterday. "I forgot to check this out. Sorry."

"Not a problem at all." Grace took the book to the circulation desk and completed the process of checking it out for him.

When she handed the book back, his eyes met

hers. For a moment, they just stood there, gazing at each other.

"I was actually hoping I could talk to you for a minute."

"Of course," she said. "What's on your mind?"

Mason hesitated for a moment before speaking. He turned his head again, giving her only one side of his face in profile. It was good she only saw one half of him. If she'd borne witness to the man's full beauty, she would have been rendered mute.

"Ms. Montgomery-"

"Grace," she interrupted. "Call me Grace. Please."

"Grace," he responded, his voice carrying a hint of vulnerability. "I just wanted to tell you... to warn you that I overheard the councilman talking to others last night at the beach. He was getting people on his side about discontinuing the reading program."

A wave of concern washed over Grace. Her shoulders slumped upon hearing the news. Just as she was building her army, it would appear that Councilman Spalding was doing the same.

"We can't let them succeed," Mason went on. "The children in this town deserve the opportunity to explore the worlds that books offer, to ignite their imagination and foster a love for reading."

Grace's heart had raced the other day when they'd touched for the first time. Now it stopped beating and swooned inside her chest. Grace had to admit it; she was a goner for this man.

"Reading has been my escape since I was a kid, my solace in the darkest of times. Every child should have that same freedom, that same chance to discover the magic within the pages."

A warmth spread through Grace's chest, resuscitating her heart as she listened to Mason's words. Her admiration for him grew as her heartbeat came back online. She admired his belief in the power of books to heal and uplift.

"Count me in," he was saying. "I'll do whatever you need to help."

"That would be amazing, Mason. What I really need is for you to help me with the kids. Teach them like you did with Emily."

It took him a moment. He chewed on the inside of his lip as he thought it over. Then, finally, he nodded his head.

"Really?"

He nodded again, turning to face her head on.

A gasp escaped Grace at the impact of the full effect of Mason Anderson.

Mason's brows drew in. He ducked his head. With slumping shoulders, he turned away from her. "Unless you think I'll scare the kids."

"Scare the kids?"

"Yeah. With this." He turned back to her. His index finger ran down the length of his cheek.

It took Grace a moment before she registered the scar there. At first, her attention lingered on his features. She was captivated by the strength and ruggedness that defined him. Those green eyes still captivated her. The strong chin and proud nose made her feel like she would swoon like a damsel of a historical romance. It took her a few heartbeats before her eyes landed on the faint trail of the scar that traversed his cheek.

To her, his scar did not detract from his striking appearance or her growing interest in him. Instead, it added a layer of depth and vulnerability that only drew her closer.

As she returned her gaze to Mason, she noticed a flicker of confusion in his eyes as if he had braced himself for a different reaction. Grace took a step closer, closing the gap between them.

"You think you'll scare the kids because you have a scar?"

He didn't answer. Not at first. His lips worked, as though trying to find a way past the wound inside of him. "I thought I scared you because of the scar."

"Honestly, I didn't notice it until you pointed it out. I was drawn to your reading material."

When Mason winced, Grace knew she'd put her foot in her mouth again.

"I mean, I like the fact that you read romance novels. It's like you're studying the manual."

"The manual?"

"For women."

"Pardon?"

"I just mean that I think a man who reads romance novels must truly understand women."

"You think *Far From the Maddening Crowd* is a romance novel?"

"Well, in comparison to *Tess of the D'Urbervilles,* yes."

A mixture of surprise and relief washed over his face, as if her words had lifted a weight from his shoulders. "Yeah. I suppose."

"I mean it's not exactly my go-to for a historical romance novel."

"Let me guess; Austen?"

"Julia Quinn or Lisa Kleypas."

"I haven't heard of either of them."

Now it was Grace's gaze that lit up in surprise. "Let me introduce you."

She turned on her heel and headed for the romance section. She didn't look back to see if he followed. She went down on her knees, sitting cross-legged to reach the Q section of the paperbacks and find the Bridgerton novels.

"Start here with *The Duke and I.*"

Mason stared down at both her and her outstretched hand with the worn novel. Slowly, he lowered himself until he was sitting next to her. He took the book from her. When his fingers brushed hers again, there was that zap of electricity between them.

Grace knew he felt it. Because this time, he inhaled sharply. Their gazes connected. He faced her full-on, showing her his full self.

"I just wanted to say that I'm sorry for how I acted yesterday," he said. "I didn't mean to be grumpy with you. It's just..."

"Don't worry about it," she said, smiling at him.

He looked down at the book they both held a corner of. "I do like romance novels. For me, it's more about the guaranteed happily ever after. After everything I've been through, it's nice to have something that I know will end well."

Grace smiled at him, feeling a sense of warmth spreading through her chest. She had always believed that books had the power to bring people together, to create connections and foster understanding. And now, as she talked to Mason about their favorite romance novels, she could see that power in action.

Maybe, just maybe, there was hope for the reading program after all. But more importantly, maybe this was the start of their own happily ever after. Grace decided to press her luck.

"I was thinking, in addition to the reading program, maybe starting up a romance novel reading club."

"Yeah? That sounds interesting. Who's invited?"

"Maybe we start small? Just the two of us?"

Grace let go of the book. But not before her fingertips lightly traced the tip of his thumb. The touch was delicate, tender, a gesture of reassurance and acceptance. She met his gaze, her eyes filled with sincerity.

"I'd love to read with you," Mason said.

A spark of something powerful passed between

them in that fleeting moment. It was the start of something. For the first time in her life, Grace didn't feel the need to skip to the end. She wanted to experience each page of this new adventure, one paragraph at a time.

CHAPTER SIX

ason stood at the beach, the salty breeze caressing his face and tousling his hair. The rhythmic crash of the waves against the shore filled his ears, mingling with the laughter of children building sandcastles and the distant calls of seagulls.

Jace and Alex joined him at the water's edge. Normally, it was Alex who got here first. After his retirement from the military, the man had been restless. He'd walked up and down the beach the first few weeks he'd come to Honor's Valley. But once he'd found Aria, the town's barista, he spent more time in her café than on the sand.

The same with Alex, who was an admitted workaholic. But after his fake relationship with the town's florist, Sarah, he was up with the sun, helping her water her peonies. Mason wasn't sure if that was a double entendre.

Though both men now arrived later, they always made a point to show up for each other. The camaraderie between them was palpable, a bond forged through shared experiences and unwavering support. Today, Mason had something he couldn't wait to share with them. Yet, a flicker of hesitation held him back.

"I finally talked to her."

"Her who?" asked Alex, always needing things to be clear and succinct.

"The librarian, Grace."

"Oh, I know Grace," said Jace. "She's Aria's best friend."

"I thought Sarah was her best friend."

"I think they're all three best friends."

Mason hadn't taken the time to meet either of his friends' new loves. His insecurities had held him back. But after spending most of the day stealing glances and grins with Grace in the stacks, he felt more and more like coming out of his shell.

Jace raised an eyebrow, a mischievous glint in his eyes. "So you and Grace? Tell us everything, man."

"There's something about her, something that draws me to her."

His two friends shared a knowing look. Mason didn't need a dictionary to interpret that look. He'd had that smug look when he'd seen them falling for the women who now held their hearts in their palms. When Mason had taken the romance novel from Grace's hands earlier, that spark he'd felt when their flesh met had been the start of his heart's surrender.

"We have a lot in common. She loves reading rom—" Mason traced the scar that marked his cheek. A wave of self-consciousness washed over him, a vulnerability he hadn't anticipated.

"What was that?" said Jace. "She likes reading about Rome?"

"I love history books about the rise and fall of Rome," said Alex.

Mason nodded, pressing his lips together. He was not about to tell his friends about his love of romance novels. They thought Thomas Hardy wrote about British history. He was glad he'd left the Julia Quinn book tucked under his pillow this morning.

He'd gone into the novel full of skepticism. But he had to admit, he was enjoying the shenanigans that Daphne and her duke were getting up to in ballrooms.

"What I mean," Mason began, "is that she told me about this incredible reading program she's fighting to save. It's amazing how passionate she is about it."

"Yeah, Aria was telling me about it last night. Let me know how I can help."

"Me, too," chimed in Alex.

"You know, Mason," said Jace, "this sounds like something you could really get behind. You've always had a way with words, man."

Alex nodded in agreement, a supportive smile on his face. "Exactly, Mason. We're here to support you, no matter what. And it's pretty cool."

With his friend's support propping him up, Mason entered the library later that afternoon. He looked around for Grace, but didn't see her. He knew she was here. He could smell the vanilla scent of the perfume she favored.

Instead of Grace, he saw a bunch of kids spread out around a table. They all looked down at their phones or gaming cards instead of at the books spread out on the table. Mason watched from the sidelines, feeling a mix of nerves and excitement.

He had never worked with kids before. Except for Emily, of course. He wasn't sure what to expect.

Mason stood before the small group of children, their eager eyes fixed on him with a mixture of curiosity and anticipation. The room buzzed with the energy of young minds ready to embark on an adventure within the pages of books. The soft glow of the reading lamps cast a warm ambiance, and the scent of freshly printed pages filled the air.

"All right, everyone," came Grace's voice. "Today, we're going to dive into the world of storytelling. I want each of you to pick a book that sparks your interest, something that ignites your imagination."

Excited whispers filled the room as the children scurried to the shelves, their tiny fingers tracing the spines of countless stories. Mason was excited at the sight of Grace. She looked even more beautiful today. The open book earrings that dangled from her ears made him smile. He wanted to pull her closer to write the start of their story on those metallic pages.

A young girl approached Grace, clutching a picture book with colorful illustrations. Her eyes glimmered with anticipation, and she held the book up to her, a silent request for approval.

Grace smiled warmly, her voice filled with encouragement. "That's a wonderful choice, Lily. Mr. Anderson will help you to read it. Won't you, Mason?"

The truth was Mason was prepared to do any and everything Grace asked of him. As they settled into a cozy reading nook, Mason utilized various techniques to engage the children, making the stories come alive. He used different voices for characters, encouraged them to visualize the scenes, and prompted them with thought-provoking questions. With each turn of the page, he witnessed their imaginations soar and their confidence in their reading abilities grow.

The room was alive with laughter, whispers, and the rustle of pages as the children eagerly shared their newfound literary discoveries. Mason reveled in their excitement, his heart swelling with pride at their progress. But he knew that it wasn't just about teaching them to read—it was about instilling a love for storytelling, a passion that would stay with them for a lifetime.

Amidst the buzz of the room, Grace watched him, her eyes shining with admiration. As the session came to a close, she approached him, a soft smile playing on her lips.

"Mason, you did an incredible job with the kids today."

Mason felt a flush of warmth spreading through his body at her words. He had waited for one of the kids to make a remark about his scar. They'd hardly even stared at it. They were so engrossed with the story he was telling them and having them read back to him.

He felt a huge sense of accomplishment. But now all he felt was a desire to be alone with Grace. Luckily, he had just what he wanted. They were alone in the library.

"You ready for this?" asked Grace.

Mason frowned, uncertain exactly what she was referring to but ready for anything she threw at him.

Grace held up a second copy of *The Duke and I.* "It's Grace and Mason book club time."

He grinned as he followed her over to the reading pillows thrown haphazardly on the floor.

"You probably haven't gotten started yet," she began, "but I figured we could read a bit together."

"I'm nearly done," he admitted.

"Done? No way."

"I'm loving Daphne and Simon and the charade of pretending to be engaged. It reminds me of my friend Alex—"

"And Sarah; yes. I'm the one that gave them the idea."

"Why am I not surprised? Of course, you would be the one to weave a tale around them about discovering the strength to follow your heart even when the path seems uncertain. Daphne and Simon's love story mirrors Alex and Sarah's because they both found someone who accepts them completely, scars and all."

A soft blush colored Grace's cheeks as she leaned in, her hand reaching toward him. Mason leaned closer, allowing her fingertips to lightly trace the path of his scar. The touch was delicate, tender, a gesture of reassurance and acceptance. She met his gaze, her eyes filled with sincerity.

"Mason, I see you for who you truly are, beyond the surface. And what I see is a remarkable person."

A spark of something powerful passed between them in that fleeting moment—a silent agreement that their connection was based on something far more profound than physical appearance. A soft smile played at the corners of Grace's lips. In that shared understanding, Mason knew what he had to do.

He leaned forward and captured Grace's smile with his own. The air crackled with an electric current, charged with the unspoken desire that had been building between them. It was as if time stood still, the world fading away to leave only the two of them in that tiny, intimate space between the library stacks.

Before his lips met hers, Mason saw the soft blush gracing Grace's cheeks, mirroring the warmth that surged through his own veins. Her lips, full and inviting, beckoned to him, whispering promises of a connection that went beyond words.

A symphony of emotions played within Mason's chest. Nervousness intertwined with the fervent desire that pulsed through his veins. Doubt mingled with a newfound sense of hope as he wondered if he was ready to take this leap, to embrace the vulnerability that came with sharing such an intimate moment.

With a trembling hand, Mason reached out and covered Grace's hand that held on to his deepest vulnerability, the wound that had almost cost him his life. He savored the sensation of her touch against his, memorizing every detail of this precious connection.

Their breaths mingled, creating a delicate dance between them. Mason's gaze flickered to Grace's lips, their softness and the promise they held becoming irresistible. He closed his eyes, surrendering to the moment, trusting that this leap of faith would bring them closer, not just physically, but on a deeper level.

And then their lips met.

A spark ignited, sending a rush of warmth and passion cascading through Mason's entire being. It was a gentle yet fervent kiss, filled with the intensity of unspoken emotions and the longing they had both held at bay. In that single, tender moment, all doubts and fears melted away, replaced by the sheer certainty that this connection was something extraordinary.

CHAPTER SEVEN

Grace was nervous as Mason picked her up for their date. They had spent so much time together working on the reading program, and she had started to develop feelings for him. But going on an official date was a whole different level.

She felt a mixture of excitement and nervousness. She had been looking forward to their date all week, and the butterflies in her stomach were making her feel giddy.

They hadn't managed to find much time alone in the library with the sudden surge in the popularity of the reading program. Mason was a hit with the kids, and they told their friends. Each afternoon, more kids showed up. Then they lingered after the reading time was over. This left very little time to steal kisses in between the stacks.

But tonight, they were headed out of the library. Mason was taking her for a night on the town. When he arrived, she stepped out of her house and greeted him with a breathless smile.

Mason stood on her doorstep, resplendent in a well-fitted suit that accentuated his broad shoulders and chiseled features. Her gaze traveled over his clean-shaven face, appreciating the attention he had put into his appearance for their special evening.

"Mason, you look incredible."

"And you're breathtaking."

Grace's cheeks flushed at his compliment, a mixture of excitement and happiness flooding her senses. He held out his hand to her, and Grace took it. In Mason's presence, she felt cherished, desired, and safe.

They entered the upscale restaurant hand in hand. Grace felt pride swell in her chest as women snuck glances at her. She couldn't blame them. She was on the arm of the handsomest man in the whole valley.

Not only was Mason a looker, he was kind and

thoughtful and smart. Best of all, he shared her appreciation of books. They were zipping through the Bridgerton saga. Mason had even convinced Grace to take another look at a Hardy novel. She had to admit that the writing was top notch, even if there weren't as many swoony scenes as a historical romance written by a modern writer.

Grace turned her attention back to the elegant atmosphere in the restaurant. The tantalizing aroma of fine cuisine enveloped them, setting the stage for a memorable evening. However, as they approached the hostess stand, Grace couldn't help but notice a subtle change in Mason's demeanor.

A flicker of unease passed across his features, causing him to duck his head ever so slightly. His usual confident stance seemed to waver, and a faint hint of self-consciousness tainted his typically strong presence. It was as if a veil of insecurity had momentarily overshadowed his spirit.

As they were shown to their table, Grace caught a glimpse of Mason turning away from the waiter, avoiding direct eye contact as they placed their orders. His gaze seemed to dart around the room, as if he believed the eyes of others were fixed upon him, judging his every move.

Grace's heart squeezed with a mixture of

concern and tenderness as she observed these subtle gestures. She had become attuned to the intricacies of Mason's emotions, understanding the depths of his wounds and the ongoing battle he faced within himself. It was clear that the scars he carried, both visible and hidden, still held the power to ignite his insecurities.

Leaning closer, she gently touched his hand, intertwining her fingers with his in a silent gesture of support. She wanted him to know that she saw him, not just the confident exterior he projected, but the vulnerable soul beneath.

"Mason," she whispered softly, her voice laced with warmth and reassurance, "I'm so happy we're doing this tonight."

His eyes met hers, a mix of gratitude and vulnerability reflected in their depths. She saw the flicker of relief as he allowed himself to be comforted by her presence, to trust in her acceptance of every facet of his being.

The soft glow of the chandelier cast a gentle ambiance around them. As they sat across from each other, their fingers intertwined. Taking a deep breath, Mason turned to face her, his eyes filled with a mix of trepidation and trust. His words spilled forth, accompanied by the weight of memories that had burdened his soul for far too long.

"The scar on my face," he began, his fingertips instinctively tracing the jagged line that marred his skin, "it's a constant reminder of a battle I fought in, one that left its mark on me, both inside and out."

Grace's eyes mirrored a gentle understanding, encouraging him to continue.

"I was deployed, serving as a language specialist. During a mission, our convoy was ambushed. I did my best to protect my unit, but the chaos of that moment... it was overwhelming."

A flicker of pain danced across his features as he recalled the harrowing memories. "I carry the guilt of surviving when others didn't," he confessed, his voice filled with raw emotion. "It's a weight I've carried for so long, questioning why it was me, why I made it out when others didn't."

Tears welled in Grace's eyes as she listened, her heart aching for the pain he had endured. "Mason," she whispered, her voice filled with compassion, "you are not defined by the scars you bear. They are a testament to your bravery and resilience. You survived, and that is something to be celebrated."

Grace's fingers gently cupped his face, her

touch a tender reassurance. "I see the man behind the scars, the heart that beats with kindness, the spirit that perseveres despite the darkness," she replied, her voice filled with unwavering conviction. "Your appearance doesn't change the way I feel about you. It only makes me cherish you more."

With each word spoken, she could see a weight lifting from Mason's shoulders. His head lifted higher, his shoulders straightening.

"Plus, I think it makes you look hot."

That startled a laugh out of him. Mason smiled at her, his eyes shining with gratitude. "You always know just what to say, Grace. You're my heroine."

Grace laughed, feeling a warmth spread through her body. "I should hope so. I'm determined to have my very own HEA."

The moment the words, or rather letters, were out of her mouth, Grace colored. She hadn't meant to be so forward. But instead of pulling away, Mason squeezed her hands with his.

"I can relate to that. After all the chaos of war, there's something reassuring about a guaranteed happily-ever-after ending."

Grace felt a thrill of excitement and possibility run through her as she looked into his eyes. She knew that there were obstacles and challenges ahead, but she felt ready to face them with Mason by her side.

"You make a difference every day, Grace," Mason said, his voice low and intense. "You inspire people to love reading and to see the world in new ways. And you've inspired me to believe in a future where anything is possible."

CHAPTER EIGHT

*M*ason took a deep breath and tried to steady his nerves as he followed Grace into the hearing room. He couldn't help but feel a sense of dread as he saw the hostile faces of the council members. He knew how these things worked—they always found a way to say no, no matter how valid the argument.

As they took their seats, Mason could feel his anxiety mounting. He tried to keep his breathing steady and focus on Grace's words, but his mind was racing with memories of his time in the service. The noise of the room was overwhelming —the sound of shuffling papers, the murmur of voices, the tapping of fingers on the table.

The room seemed to close in around him,

reminiscent of being on a battlefield when the enemy had surrounded him and his unit. He had to remind himself that he wasn't out in the desert any longer. He was back on home soil. But it didn't feel like he was on friendly turf.

As his eyes scanned the council members, he felt their scrutiny piercing through him. Their skeptical gazes fixating on his presence alongside Grace. As Grace began her argument, he tried to tune out the distractions and focus on her words.

The event was sparsely attended. Jace was helping Aria with a repair at the coffee shop. Alex was attending a work event with Sarah. Mostly, there were just the men and women sitting on a low platform and a few people seated in the folded chairs on the opposite side of the room.

When the head of the council began to speak, Mason felt his anxiety spike. The man's voice was grating, and his words were clearly meant to undermine Grace's position.

"Ms. Montgomery, we have received your proposal for the reading program," the head of the council began, his voice cool and businesslike. "While we appreciate your enthusiasm, we simply cannot justify the expense of this program at this time."

"Mr. Spalding, the reading program is so important for the children in our town," Grace said, her voice cool despite her balled fists. "It's been proven time and again that reading is essential for their development and their future success."

"Ms. Montgomery, we understand your passion, but the fact remains that our town is facing some serious financial challenges. We simply cannot afford to fund every pet project that comes along."

"I understand that times are tough, but I truly believe that this program could make a real difference in our community," she said, her voice shaking slightly. "I've taken on a volunteer to help me out. I just need the budget for materials."

Mr. Spalding held up his finger. "A volunteer? We didn't approve anyone."

Mr. Spalding's gaze landed on Mason. His beady eyes narrowed. Mason could see the wheels turning in the man's mind, recalling their interaction at the beach last week.

"Him?" the man sneered.

"Yes, him," said Grace. "Mason Anderson served his country, and now he's come home to serve his community."

"I think that man has serious behavioral issues."

Spalding's voice dripped with disdain. "But furthermore, I don't see why a stranger to our community should have any say in our community programs."

Mason's jaw tightened as he felt the need to justify himself, to prove that he had something valuable to offer. The old wounds of judgment and prejudice resurfaced, threatening to consume him.

But as the questioning continued, Grace stepped in, her voice steady and unwavering. She passionately defended Mason's involvement, high-lighting the positive impact he had made on the children, their enthusiasm for learning reignited under his guidance.

"He may not have the conventional background you're expecting, but he has a genuine passion for helping these children," Grace asserted, her voice filled with determination.

Grace's unwavering support and her belief in his abilities fueled a spark of confidence within him. With a steadying breath, Mason found his voice, each word laced with the weight of his conviction.

"I've seen firsthand the impact of this program on these children's lives. I've seen their confidence grow, their love for reading ignited. I believe in the power of kids being able to read on their own, and I am committed to helping them succeed. It would be wrong to end this program."

"Is that a threat, Mr. Anderson?"

The room fell into a silence as Mr. Spalding and Mason faced off. It was Mason's hands that now balled into fists. A few gazes dipped to catch the movement. A triumphant smile played across Spalding's face from his place up on the small platform surrounded by the other members.

Mason struggled to keep his composure. He felt like he was suffocating, trapped in this room with all these people who seemed determined to make things difficult for him and Grace. He wanted to run, to escape, but he knew he couldn't.

Mason opened his mouth to respond, but Spalding beat him to it.

"There is a discretionary fund that we could squeeze a few dollars out of for materials, Ms. Montgomery. But you'll have to assure the council that you'll only use volunteers from our approved list."

Meaning not Mason.

CHAPTER NINE

Grace's heart sank as she realized the gravity of the situation before her. Mr. Spalding had cunningly cornered her, forcing her to make an impossible choice between the reading program she had fought so hard to protect and the man who had become an unexpected source of solace and love in her life. Her gaze shifted to Mr. Spalding, his smug expression etched across his face, relishing the power he held over her.

She looked around the room at the other council members, hoping to find a spark of empathy or a glimmer of support. But their hesitant expressions betrayed their uncertainty, their fear of standing up against the dominant force of Mr. Spalding's influence.

In her desperation, Grace turned around, seeking Mason's presence, only to find an empty space where he had stood just moments ago. Panic seized her heart as she realized that he had left, likely unable to bear the weight of the situation and the possibility of being the reason for the program's demise.

Devastation washed over Grace. She felt the weight of the council's decision pressing down on her shoulders, the crushing reality of having to choose between her passion for literacy and the burgeoning love she had found in Mason's arms. It was a choice she never wanted to make.

In that moment of profound sadness, Grace's determination flickered to life. She could not let Mr. Spalding's manipulative tactics and the council's silence dictate the course of her life or the fate of the children she had come to care for deeply.

Grace straightened her shoulders and looked Mr. Spalding directly in the eye. Her voice, though tinged with sadness, rang out with a strength she didn't know she possessed. "I refuse to let you tear apart something that means so much to these children, to this community. This is not over."

Her words hung in the air, a defiant declaration of her unwavering commitment. Though she was devastated by Mason's absence, she would not let it overshadow the resilience within her. She would fight for what she believed in, and he was one of those things. But the reading program would have to take precedence right now.

Outside in the cool evening, the air was heavy with disappointment and resignation. Before she took the first step toward the library, a hand gently rested on her shoulder, halting her steps. Turning around, she found herself face to face with one of the council members, who had remained silent during the ordeal. Carl Syme looked down at her with a glimmer of sympathy in his eyes, a hint of compassion that gave her a sliver of hope.

"I agree with you, Grace."

"Didn't sound like it in there."

Carl sighed. "Spalding can be… Listen, if you can rally the community behind you, if you can show them the impact and importance of the reading program, there might be a chance to reverse this decision."

Grace knew many of the townspeople wanted the reading program. They'd told her as much. But they hadn't shown up tonight.

"Start a petition," Carl said. "If you can get enough signatures, that should be enough."

Grace gave him a nod. She turned on her heel and headed down the street. With a renewed determination, she set her sights on the task ahead. She would reach out to the community, share her passion, and show them the true value of the reading program. It wouldn't be an easy journey, but she had faith that together, they could over-turn the council's decision and secure a brighter future for the children she cared so deeply about.

And then there was Mason. She had grown so close to him over the past few days. They had bonded over their love of books and their shared desire to help the children in the community. But now if the program ended, she could lose him too. It was too much to bear.

She felt a sense of urgency to find Mason and show him that he was worth fighting for. She knew that he had left the town hall meeting out of guilt and a belief that his presence would only hinder her cause. But Grace was determined to prove him wrong, to demonstrate that their connection ran deeper than any decision the council could make.

With a determined stride, Grace made her way

through the streets of the small town, her mind consumed with thoughts of Mason and the impact he had already made on her life. She knew that she needed to find a way to reach him, to convince him that their connection was strong enough to withstand the challenges they faced.

CHAPTER TEN

The morning sunlight filtered through the curtains, casting a soft glow in Mason's room as he stirred from a restless sleep. His mind was heavy with thoughts of the previous night's events. An ache settled in his chest as he felt the absence of Grace in his heart.

How had she gotten in there so quickly? The organ beat sluggishly with the knowledge that he'd have to keep his distance if he wanted her to keep the reading program—and probably her job. He'd have to be the one to give up the safe space of the library, the fulfilling work of working with the kids, and the woman he had admittedly fallen in love with.

As he lay there, his thoughts tangled in a web of

self-doubt and longing, Mason couldn't help but reflect on the choices he had made. He had spent so much of his life hiding, concealing both his physical scars and the emotional wounds he carried deep within. And now, once again, he found himself retreating into the shadows, consumed by the guilt of the pain he had caused.

A sigh escaped his lips, the weight of his past burdens pressing down on him. He had come to care for Grace deeply, to cherish the connection they had formed. Yet he couldn't help but question if he deserved her, if he was capable of truly being the partner she deserved.

With a heavy heart, Mason swung his legs over the edge of the bed and rose to his feet. As he moved through the morning routine, the mirror became an unwelcome reflection of his doubts and insecurities. His scarred face stared back at him, a stark reminder of the battles he had fought and the losses he had endured.

It was late in the morning when Mason made his way out of the house. His sister, her husband, and Emily had long since left and gotten their day started. Mason started toward the library, but his feet wouldn't let him go that route. He still wasn't convinced that his presence there would help Grace or the program. Instead, he sought out his favorite bench on the beach.

As the sun dipped below the horizon, casting a golden glow over the beach, Mason found solace in the rhythm of the rolling waves. The ebb and flow of the tide mirrored the tumultuous emotions swirling within him.

Lost in his thoughts, Mason didn't notice the approaching footsteps until a chorus of young voices called out his name. Startled, he turned to find the kids from the reading program standing before him.

"Mr. Anderson, we need your help," one of the children, Sally, said, her voice laced with urgency.

Mason's first thought was that something had happened to Grace. He sprang to his feet, already in motion toward the library. But Sally's small hand stopped him.

"We heard that they're getting rid of the after-school reading program. Can you believe that?"

Mason pursed his lips. He was still on pins and needles at the thought of Grace being in trouble. It took all of his concentration to focus on the children.

"Ms. Montgomery stopped by summer school

today to collect something called signatures. Do you know what that is?"

Sally handed over a document to Mason. It was a petition to save the reading program. It looked like she was going to fight.

Of course she was. She was Grace. He remembered how she'd barred his way out of the door when she'd asked for his help.

"We want to help too. We just don't know what a signature is."

Mason looked at the earnest faces before him, their innocence and trust shining through. He couldn't help but be moved by their unwavering belief in the power of the written word and the impact the reading program had on their lives.

If Grace was out there, gathering signatures, then he wanted to be there too.

Mason and the children ventured through the neighborhood, going from door to door to collect signatures. He stood at the back and let the kids lead as they explained the importance of the reading program to each neighbor they encountered.

In the midst of their efforts, Mason felt a gentle tap on his shoulder. Turning, he found himself face to face with Mrs. Garcia, one of the mothers from the reading program, her eyes shimmering with gratitude and admiration.

"Mason," she began, her voice filled with sincerity, "I wanted to thank you for all the help you've given my child. Ever since he joined the reading program, his confidence has soared, and his love for books has grown by leaps and bounds."

A warmth spread through Mason's chest, a validation of the impact he had made on this young reader's life. He had often doubted his worth, questioning whether he had the ability to make a difference. But this mother's heartfelt appreciation reminded him that his presence, support, and dedication mattered.

Mason felt a warmth spread through him at her words. "It's been my pleasure," he said, looking down at the boy, who was beaming up at him. "He's a great kid, and he's been working really hard."

"Please know that you are making a difference, not just in my child's life, but in the lives of all the children in this program. We are grateful for you and Grace, and you both have our unwavering support."

The weight of Mason's own insecurities seemed to momentarily lift as he stood there, connecting with this mother on a profound level. It was a reminder that the scars he carried didn't define him. Rather, it was the impact he could make, the connections he could forge, and the love he could share that truly mattered.

"Well, I wanted to let you know that I'll be speaking to the council about the reading program," Mrs. Garcia continued. "I think it's so important for kids like my son to have access to programs like this."

"Thank you, Mrs. Garcia," he said. "That means a lot."

As Mrs. Garcia left, Mason turned back to the kids. He realized that he needed to do more than just help out with the program—he needed to fight for Grace. He looked at the two kids, who were both looking up at him with wide eyes.

"Guys," he said, "I need your help with something."

CHAPTER ELEVEN

Grace walked along the familiar streets of her hometown. She'd spent her entire life in Honor's Valley, not wanting to stray far from the familiar. Books were the places she went to escape.

Now when her footsteps took her down paths known to her, she felt completely out of step with reality. The weight of the petition in her hands mirrored the burden that settled on her heart. She had been tirelessly collecting signatures, but the number seemed insufficient to sway the council's decision.

Aside from that, she hadn't heard from Mason. He hadn't shown up at the library this morning. He hadn't called or texted her. He hadn't responded to any of her calls or texts.

Well, enough was enough. Grace wasn't a historical damsel. She was a modern woman, and she was taking matters into her own hands.

He might think he was being a hero by backing away from her so that she wouldn't have to choose between him and the reading program. But the choice was a false equivalency. She was going to fight to keep both.

As she approached Mason's sister's house, her steps quickened, hope mingling with apprehension. She needed to find Mason, to see him, and to share the weight of this endeavor with him. But when she reached the front door and knocked, it was Mary Ellen who greeted her with a somber expression.

"Grace," Mary Ellen said softly, concern etching lines on her face, "I haven't seen Mason all morning. He usually spends his days at the library."

Grace knew he wasn't there. When he hadn't shown up this morning, she'd put a temporarily closed sign on the front door and went out to collect signatures with the two other part-time librarians and a couple of volunteer workers.

"Is everything okay?" Mary Ellen asked, her

gaze searching Grace's face. "You seem worried. Are you and Mason...?"

Mary Ellen's face lit up at the unspoken query. Were Grace and Mason...? How to fill in that sentence?

Were they dating? Were they in a relationship? Were they soul mates? Could the answer be all of the above?

Grace paused, her voice catching in her throat. How could she explain the complexity of her feelings, the uncertainty that lingered in her heart? She hadn't even defined their relationship, and yet the absence of his presence left an ache within her.

"We're... we're friends," Grace finally managed to say, her voice tinged with a mix of sadness and longing. "But I haven't heard from him today. I thought he would be here, supporting the cause."

Mary Ellen's gaze landed on the petition. "He didn't tell me he was working on the reading program. It makes sense since he loves books. You know, I even found a few romance novels in his room. Don't tell him that, though. He'll be embarrassed."

Mary Ellen chuckled as she took the petition from Grace and added her signature.

"I know he'll want to sign this too," she continued. "Mason has his demons, his battles. Sometimes, they consume him. But reading has always been an escape for him. He'll want to join this fight."

Grace nodded, her fingers gripping the petition tighter as she tried to regain her composure. "Thank you, Mary Ellen," she said, her voice filled with gratitude. "If you find him, tell him... tell him I need him, and I won't give up."

Mary Ellen's lips parted. Understanding began to dawn in her eyes, but Grace turned and began walking away.

As she walked away, Mary Ellen's words lingered in her mind, echoing with the promise of a love that could weather the storms of doubt and insecurity. Grace clung to that hope, a beacon guiding her forward as she forged ahead, determined to make a difference and to prove that love, even in its most challenging moments, could overcome all obstacles.

When she came up to the library with key in hand to unlock the door, she found a veritable crowd gathered outside the door. There were mostly kids standing on the sidewalk. They held signs in crayon colors demanding neighbors' signatures. Plenty of neighbors were stopping to do just as the kids commanded.

"We've got more than enough signatures already," said a deep voice from behind her.

Grace turned to find Mason standing behind her. He looked down at her with a mix of determination and apology.

"I know I let you down before, Grace," Mason said, his voice strong and clear. "But I'm here now, and I'm not leaving until we save this program."

Grace felt her eyes fill with tears as she realized what he had done. He had rallied the community to stand up for the reading program and for her. She took a deep breath and his hand as she looked out at the crowd of parents and children, feeling overwhelmed with gratitude and emotion.

"I want to thank all of you for being here," Grace said, her voice trembling with emotion. "This program means so much to me, and I'm so grateful to all of you for your support."

The parents and children cheered, and Grace felt a wave of relief and hope wash over her. She knew that with this kind of community support, they could save the reading program and keep it going for years to come.

At her side, Mason gave her hand a squeeze. He

had turned to face her, giving her his scarred side. But then he turned to face the crowd head-on. In that moment, she knew that no matter what the future held, they would face it together, as a team.

"We're here to stand with Grace and the reading program she's created for these kids," he said. "I have personally seen the progress your children have made, and I know that this program is making a difference in their lives. I'm willing to offer one-on-one help. All we're asking you to do is show your support with a signature."

More people came from across the street to add the names and their voices to the cause. A few shared their own stories of how their children, or even they themselves, struggled with reading.

As the crowd focused on the clipboards, Mason turned to Grace.

"I realize now that I made a mistake by not standing up for both you and the reading program last night. I was afraid and let my own issues get in the way. But I've seen firsthand how much this program means to these kids, and I don't want to see it taken away."

Mason swallowed. The lump in his throat was audible, and he had to swallow again before more words came out.

"I see how important you are to me, and I'm not letting you get away, either."

Grace smiled. Then she giggled. Then she laughed.

"What's so funny?" Mason asked.

"You actually thought you had a choice? You thought I was letting such an amazing man like you get away? You do realize this is a small town with few dating prospects."

Grace wrapped her arms around Mason's neck. She twined her fingers, locking them together. Mason seemed in no hurry to escape. This was the moment she had been waiting for, a moment that held the power to redefine their relationship and solidify their love.

As Mason began speaking, his voice carrying a weight of past insecurities and self-doubt, Grace's heart ached for him. She had glimpsed the pain behind his eyes, the walls he had built to protect himself from further hurt. But now, he stood before her, laying bare his deepest fears and opening himself up to her completely.

"I used to believe that my scars made me unlovable." Mason's voice trembled slightly, his eyes searching hers for understanding. "The battles I fought, both seen and unseen, left their mark on me. They created wounds that ran deeper than the surface."

She listened intently, her love for him only growing stronger with each word he spoke. Grace knew that beneath the scars, the emotional turmoil, and the haunting memories lay a man of immeasurable strength and resilience.

"But you, Grace, have shattered those beliefs. Your kindness has shown me that I am more than my scars, more than the pain I've endured. Through your eyes, I've learned to see myself differently. You've given me the gift of acceptance, of feeling worthy of love."

Grace's eyes glistened with unshed tears, her heart swelling with an overwhelming love for this remarkable man standing before her. She reached out, her hand trembling slightly as it found its place in his, offering comfort and support.

"Mason, you are so much more than your scars. They tell a story of resilience, of the battles you've fought and the strength that lies within you. I love you, Mason, for the person you are, scars and all."

CHAPTER TWELVE

Mason stood before the town council. His heart was pounding. Not out of fear. His heart raced every day recently with Grace at his side. Beside him, Grace stood tall, her unwavering presence filling him with strength. They held in their hands the culmination of their efforts—the stack of signatures collected from passionate community members who believed in the power of the reading program.

"This matter isn't on the agenda today."

As Councilman Spalding's dismissive words filled the room, Mason felt a flicker of anger ignite within him. How could someone be so blind to the importance of nurturing young minds, of fostering a love for reading? He glanced at the crowd standing behind him and Grace, their faces resolute, their voices ready to be heard.

Grace took a deep breath and stepped forward. Mason, drawing upon the courage he had found within himself, stood at the ready at her back. He wasn't alone. The weight of the community's trust was warm at his back.

Grace's voice resonated with a newfound clarity and conviction. "Councilman Spalding, the signatures we bring before you today represent not just the desires of a few individuals, but the collective voice of our community. This program has touched the lives of countless children, as well as their parents. They've put their names to this petition to demand that the program not only remain but get the full funding the community believes it deserves."

The room buzzed with tension, the air thick with anticipation. Mason's gaze met Councilman Spalding's, and he saw the flicker of resistance in his eyes. The man could try to hold his ground, but the community wouldn't back down.

And then, as if orchestrated by fate itself, a voice rose from the crowd—a clear, unwavering voice that echoed through the chamber. Mason turned, his eyes widening with surprise and gratitude. It was Mrs. Ackerling, a respected member of the community, holding up another petition—a petition to have Councilman Spalding removed from office.

"I stand with Mason and Grace," Mrs. Ackerling's voice rang out, her unwavering determination inspiring those around her. "The community deserves a council that listens, that supports the growth and education of our children. Councilman Spalding's resistance to the reading program is a disservice to our town."

Grace turned to Mason, her shoulders back, her head high. They weren't alone in this fight. The community stood united, ready to challenge the status quo and demand change for the better.

With each passing moment, the voices in the crowd grew louder, joining in unison to support the reading program. The room filled with the undeniable energy of unity, a force that could not be ignored.

Mason turned back to face Councilman Spalding, his eyes filled with a steely resolve. "Councilman, you should reconsider. Look at the faces before you, the voices echoing in this room. The future of our community lies in their hands, and it's our responsibility to give them every opportunity to thrive."

Councilman Spalding's expression wavered, a moment of uncertainty crossing his features. No one sitting to his right or left offered a single word of support for him. The weight of the community's passion bore down upon him, a force that demanded change.

Finally, another councilman leaned forward and spoke into the mic. "We will revisit the funding for the reading program and consider its importance to our community. I think that this time, the community will be pleased with the outcome of the council's decision."

A cheer went up through the crowd. Grace flew into his arms. Mason caught her and held her to him. They'd done it!

Mason felt a surge of relief wash over him, knowing that their efforts had made a difference. The battle was far from over, but they had taken a significant step forward, shifting the tides in favor of the reading program and the children who depended on it.

They had fought together, faced the resistance, and emerged victorious, stronger than ever. Mason couldn't contain the overwhelming surge of joy within him. The weight of the battle lifted from his shoulders, leaving behind only a fierce sense of accomplishment and newfound hope.

With a tender smile, Mason stepped closer to the woman who held his heart. In that moment, the world around them faded into the background, leaving only the undeniable connection that had blossomed between them. He cupped her face gently in his hands, his fingers tracing the contours of her cheek.

He leaned in, his lips meeting hers in a kiss that spoke of their shared passion, their unspoken desires, and the promise of a future filled with love and endless possibilities.

Their kiss was an embrace of all that they had overcome, a celebration of their shared victory and the beginning of a beautiful love story that would continue to unfold with each passing day. In that moment, Mason knew that he had found not only a partner in life, but also a kindred spirit who understood the depths of his soul.

They stood there, connected on a profound level, their love a beacon of hope and strength. In that embrace, surrounded by the power of their love, they signed this deal with a kiss. As the kiss deepened, the pages of their happy ending came together. Their love story told the tale of healing, acceptance, and unyielding support. The sequel to their romance got its start. The beginning of the second tome started with prose of how they would face the world, knowing that their love had the strength to overcome any obstacle and rewrite the narratives of their past.

This love was not just a fleeting chapter in their lives but the beginning of a lifelong adventure filled with laughter, support, and the unwavering belief that love can truly conquer all. Hand in hand, Mason and Grace stepped into the future, ready to write the next chapters of their love story, knowing that as long as they faced the world together, their happily ever after would be nothing short of extraordinary.

Don't miss the next book in the Honor Valley Romances!

With an uneven stride, can he waltz his way into her heart?

. . .

With his injured leg, Zack Thorn is assigned to a desk job that puts him in charge of base events. Feeling sidelined due to his injury, his life takes a vibrant turn when he crosses paths with Lily Bennett, a talented dancer teaching classes on the base. As the new events coordinator, it's Zack who'll determine if she can permanently have the space on the base to hold her dance classes. But it's his heart that demands he twirl this amazing woman in his arms.

Lily Bennett is on a mission. With her heart set on a permanent place for her dance classes on the base, she's determined to use her upcoming recital to prove her worth. But when her fiery spirit catches the eye of the enigmatic Zack, she finds herself in a whirlwind of emotion that goes beyond the dance floor. She'll have to waltz past nosey dance moms and a temperamental dance partner, before she can decide if Zack should have a place on her dance card.

When their personal and professional lives get entangled in an intricate dance, Lily and Zack find themselves at a crossroads. Can Zack embrace his vulnerability and change his rhythm to match Lily's? Will Lily trust Zack's intentions and let him take the lead?

Soldier's Embrace **is a heartwarming small town, military romance that explores the power of love, growth, and healing. With the office romance, wounded hero, and fish out of water tropes at its core, this story will sweep you away and leave you rooting for Lily and Zack's happily ever after.**

Shanae Johnson was raised by Saturday Morning cartoons and After School Specials. She still doesn't understand why there isn't a life lesson that ties the issues of the day together just before bedtime. While she's still waiting for the meaning of it all, she writes stories to try and figure it all out. Her books are wholesome and sweet, but her are heroes are hot and heroines are full of sass!

And by the way, the E elongates the A. So it's pronounced Shan-aaaaaaaa. Perfect for a hero to call out across the moors, or up to a balcony, or to blare outside her window on a boombox. If you hear him calling her name, please send him her way!

You can sign up for Shanae's Reader Group and receive a FREE NOVELLA in this world at

https://shanaejohnson.com/ReaderGroup

ALSO BY SHANAE JOHNSON

Honor Valley Romances

Soldier's Surrender

Soldier's Promise

Soldier's Courage

Soldier's Embrace

Soldier's Protection

Soldier's Triumph

The Brides of Purple Heart

On His Bended Knee

Hand Over His Heart

Offering His Arm

His Permanent Scar

Having His Back

In Over His Head

Always On His Mind

Every Step He Takes

In His Good Hands

Light Up His Life

Strength to Stand

His Grace Under Pressure

The Rangers of Purple Heart

The Rancher takes his Convenient Bride

The Rancher takes his Best Friend's Sister

The Rancher takes his Runaway Bride

The Rancher takes his Star Crossed Love

The Rancher takes his Love at First Sight

The Rancher takes his Last Chance at Love

The Silver Star Ranch Romances

His Pledge to Honor

His Pledge to Cherish

His Pledge to Protect

His Pledge to Obey

His Pledge to Have

His Pledge to Hold

a Flying Cross Ranch Romance

His Vow to Love

His Vow to Treasure

His Vow to Adore

His Vow to Trust

His Vow to Respect

His Vow to Defend

Bronze Star Ranch Romance

His Duty to Serve

His Duty to Accept

His to Fulfill